The Urbana Free Library

To renew: call **217-367-4057**
or go to **urbanafreelibrary.org**
and select **My Account**

Topic: Health   **Subtopic:** Food Allergies

Notes to Parents and Teachers:

As a child becomes more familiar reading books, it is important for him/her to rely on and use reading strategies more independently to help figure out words they do not know.

REMEMBER: PRAISE IS A GREAT MOTIVATOR!

Here are some praise points for beginning readers:
• I saw you get your mouth ready to say the first letter of that word.
• I like the way you used the picture to help you figure out that word.
• I noticed that you saw some sight words you knew how to read!

Book Ends for the Reader!

Here are some reminders before reading the text:

• Point to each word you read to make it match what you say.

• Use the picture for help.

• Look at and say the first letter sound of the word.

• Look for sight words that you know how to read in the story.

• Think about the story to see what word might make sense.

Words to Know Before You Read

bake

cake

eggs

flour

food

gift

milk

sick

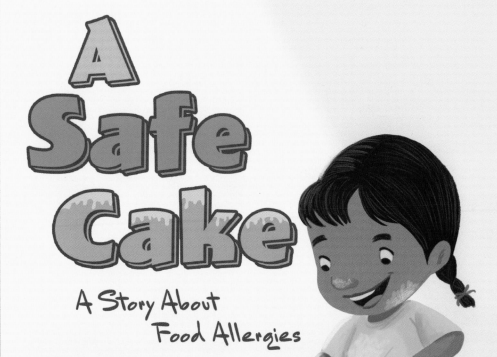

A Safe Cake

A Story About Food Allergies

By
J. L. Anderson

Illustrated by
Nadia Ronquillo

Rourke
Educational Media

rourkeeducationalmedia.com

Mia wants to give Miss Rose a gift.

Mia could bake a cake!

Cakes are yummy.

Mia grabs flour.

Then she gets eggs.

She pours some milk.

"Oops!"

Mia remembers something.

Miss Rose has a food allergy. Some foods make her sick.

Is it the flour?

Is it the eggs?

Is it the milk?

Mia is not sure.

She can eat those things. Some people can't.

Mia does not want Miss Rose to be sick.

She wants Miss Rose to feel good.
She draws a picture.

The cake looks yummy!

Miss Rose will like the gift.

Book Ends for the Reader

I know...

1. What can happen if someone has a food allergy?
2. What kind of cake does Mia make for Miss Rose?
3. Why did she decide to make this kind of cake?

I think...

1. Do you know anyone with a food allergy?

2. Why is it important not to give someone food they are allergic to?

3. Name one way people can help others with food allergies.

Book Ends for the Reader

What happened in this book?

Look at each picture and talk about what happened in the story.

About the Author

J.L. Anderson lives in Texas with her family and two dogs. She loves taking her daughter to the park and reading stories together! She has food allergies. You can learn more by visiting www.jessicaleeanderson.com.

About the Illustrator

Nadia Ronquillo was born and raised in Guayaquil, Ecuador. Ever since she could remember, she had a pencil in her hand. She spent her entire childhood drawing and painting in coloring books or sketchbooks.

Library of Congress PCN Data

A Safe Cake (A Story About Food Allergies)/J.L. Anderson
(Changes and Challenges In My Life)
ISBN 978-1-64156-499-1 (hard cover)(alk. paper)
ISBN 978-1-64156-625-4 (soft cover)
ISBN 978-1-64156-736-7 (e-Book)
Library of Congress Control Number: 2018930716

Rourke Educational Media
Printed in the United States of America,
North Mankato, Minnesota

www.rourkeeducationalmedia.com

Edited by: Keli Sipperley
Layout by: Corey Mills
Cover and interior illustrations by: John Joseph